MERRY CHRISTMAS,

SPACE CASE

by JAMES MARSHALL

DIAL BOOKS FOR YOUNG READERS · NEW YORK

To Christian, Juretta, and Travis

3 1116 01674 6486

Published by Dial Books for Young Readers · A Division of Penguin Books USA Inc.
2 Park Avenue · New York, New York 10016
Published simultaneously in Canada by Fitzhenry & Whiteside Limited, Toronto

Library of Congress Catalog Card Number: 85-1664
Printed in Hong Kong by South China Printing Company (1988) Limited
First Pied Piper Printing 1989
E
1 3 5 7 9 10 8 6 4 2

A Pied Piper Book is a registered trademark of
Dial Books for Young Readers,
a division of Penguin Books USA Inc.,
® TM 1,163,686 and ® TM 1,054,312.

MERRY CHRISTMAS, SPACE CASE
is published in a hardcover edition by
Dial Books for Young Readers.
ISBN 0-8037-0653-7

The process art consists of black line-drawings, black halftones,
and full-color washes. The black line is prepared and photographed separately
for greater contrast and sharpness. The full-color washes and black halftones
are prepared with watercolor on the reverse side of the black-line drawing.
They are then color-separated and reproduced
as red, blue, yellow, and black halftones.

Two days before Christmas Buddy McGee's dad
made a surprise announcement.
"This year we're spending Christmas at Grannie's."

"But we can't," cried Buddy. "My friend from outer space
   is coming here for Christmas."
"Not that again," said Dad.
"But it's *true*," said Buddy. "It came for a visit
   last Halloween, and it promised to come back for Christmas."
"If you say so," said Dad.
"You can leave your little friend a note," said Mom.
"But, but . . ." said Buddy.
   But that was that.
   And on Christmas Eve the McGees went to Grannie's.

"Guess what, Grannie!" said Buddy. "The thing
  from outer space is coming to your house for Christmas."
"Oh, goody," said Grannie. "Does it know the way?"
"I left it directions," said Buddy. "And it is *very* smart."
"While you're waiting for it," said Grannie, "why don't
  you play with the nice boys next door?"

But the Goober twins were not nice.

"We're getting expensive presents for Christmas," they said.

"And you're going to feel really left out."

"Oh, no I won't," said Buddy. "*I* have a friend coming
all the way from outer space for Christmas."

"You must think we're really dumb," said the Goobers.

"You'll see," said Buddy.

"If you're lying, you'll be sorry," said the Goobers.

"Uh-oh," thought Buddy.

On Christmas morning Buddy sailed downstairs.
"Maybe it's waiting for me in the living room."
But there was nothing from outer space there.
"Outer space is a long way away," said Grannie.
"Maybe it just miscalculated."
"Maybe it just forgot," said Buddy.
Suddenly from the front yard came a loud
BEEP BEEP BEEP.
"It's here!" cried Buddy.

But it was only the Goobers on their expensive
new bicycles.

"Well, where is it?" they said.

"Er," said Buddy. "It will be here."

"Your time is running out, McGee," said the Goobers.

"We don't like wise guys."

"Gosh," thought Buddy, "the thing had better
get here soon."

At that moment, a few zillion miles away, the thing from outer space was attending a wild party. Suddenly it remembered something important. "I'm going to be late for Christmas at Buddy's!" it beeped.

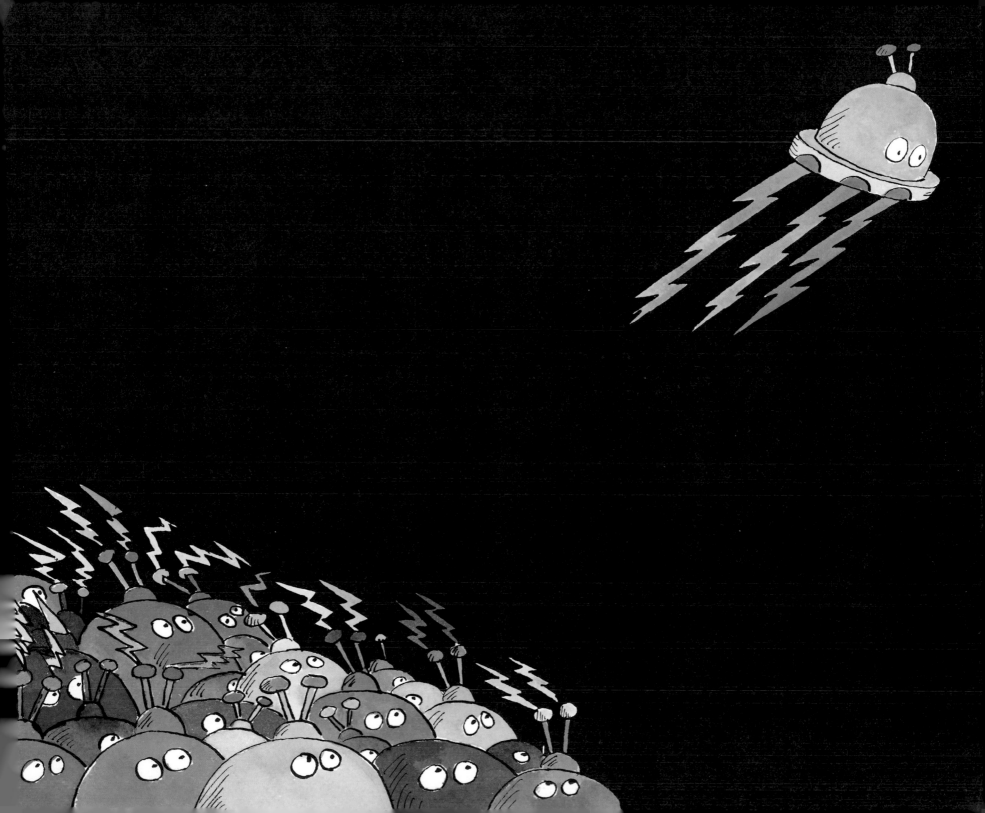

In a flash the thing was on earth—but nothing looked familiar.

The natives didn't seem to have the right Christmas spirit.

They moved closer.

"Merry Christmas," beeped the thing.

The thing got out of there fast, headed north,
and finally found Buddy's house.
It was surprised to find no one at home.
"Perhaps the next door neighbor can tell me
where they've gone," it beeped.
But the next door neighbor didn't seem
to know very much.

Returning to the McGees' house to wait, the thing
spotted Buddy's note.
"Holy smoke!" it beeped. "I'd better hurry!"
But it didn't get very far.
"Shame, shame," said the man in the blue uniform.
"Speeding—and on Christmas too."
"It won't happen again," beeped the thing.
"Fancy foreign cars," grumbled the man.

A few blocks away from Grannie's something attracted
the thing's attention.

"Hmm," it beeped. "Perhaps I can spare a moment."

And it went inside the movie theater.

Halfway through the movie, which was *very* entertaining,
the thing had a funny feeling.

"Buddy's in trouble, I just know it!"

And it blasted out of the theater.

Faster than the speed of light, it flew to Grannie's.

Buddy *was* in trouble.

"Your time is up, McGee," said the Goobers.

And they stepped closer.

Buddy's heart was pounding.

But before the Goobers could get ugly . . .

they found themselves turned into giant snowmen.
"Say you're sorry," beeped the thing.

The Goobers said they were sorry, and the thing changed
them back into the two rotten kids they were before.
"Wow," said Buddy. "Am I glad to see you."
"Likewise," beeped the thing.

Grannie and the thing got along well.
They talked a lot about science.
And after a big Christmas dinner,
while Mom and Dad were taking a snooze,
the thing took Buddy for a ride.
"Step on it!" cried Buddy.
"My turn next," called out Grannie.
Buddy and the thing had a fine time
flying over the neighborhood. . . .

And just for the heck of it, they chased the Goobers
around the block three times.